Wilhelm Richard Wagner, Charles Henry Meltzer, F. Corder

Parsifal

A Festival-Drama

Wilhelm Richard Wagner, Charles Henry Meltzer, F. Corder

Parsifal
A Festival-Drama

ISBN/EAN: 9783337376901

Printed in Europe, USA, Canada, Australia, Japan

Cover: Foto ©Andreas Hilbeck / pixelio.de

More available books at **www.hansebooks.com**

PARSIFAL.

A FESTIVAL-DRAMA

BY

RICHARD WAGNER.

TRANSLATED INTO ENGLISH IN EXACT ACCORDANCE
WITH THE ORIGINAL

BY

H. L. AND F. CORDER.

MAYENCE.

B. SCHOTT'S SÖHNE.

LONDON.	PARIS.	BRUSSELS.
SCHOTT & Co.	MAISON SCHOTT.	SCHOTT FRÈRES.
	ENT. STA. HALL.	

CHARACTERS.

AMFORTAS.
TITUREL.
GURNEMAN2
PARSIFAL.
KLINGSOR.
KUNDRY.

Knights of the Grail and Esquires. — Klingsor's Fairie
Maidens.

The scene is laid — first in the domain and in the castle of the
Grail's keepers, "Monsalvat," the country in the character of the
northern mountains of Gothic Spain: — afterwards in KLINGSOR'S
magic castle on the southern slope of the same mountains, supposed
to face Arabian Spain. — The costume of the Knights and Esquires
resembles that of the Templars: white tunic and mantle; instead
of the red cross, however, a soaring dove is represented on
scutcheon and mantle.

ACT I.

A Forest, shadowy and impressive, but not gloomy. Rock-strewn ground. A glade in the middle. L. rises the way to the Grail's castle. The ground sinks in the middle at back to a low-lying forest lake. — Day dawn — GURNEMANZ (an old but vigorous man) and two ESQUIRES (tender youths) are ensconced asleep under a tree. From L. as if from the castle, rises the solemn morning reveille of trombones.

GURNEMANZ
(waking, and shaking the ESQUIRES).

Hey! Ho! Wood-keepers twain!
Sleep-keepers I deem ye!
At least be moving with morning!
(The two ESQUIRES spring up, and then immediately sink on their knees again, ashamed.)
Hear ye the call? Now thank the Lord.
That ye are called in time to hear it.
(He also falls on his knees with them; they offer up a silent morning prayer together; when the trombones have ceased, they rise again.)
Now up, young vassals; see to the bath;
'Tis time to wait there for our monarch:
Already I behold approach
Runners before his litter bed.
(Two KNIGHTS enter from the castle.)
Hail, both! How goes Amfortas' health?
He craves to-day his bath right early:
　The simple that Gawaine
With bravest craft did win for him,
I'm hopeful it hath brought relief?

FIRST KNIGHT.

Thou knowest all and still canst hope?
　With keener smart than before

Full soon his pain returned:
Sleepless from strong oppression,
His bath he bade us to prepare.

GURNEMANZ
(drooping his head sorrowfully).

Fools are we, alleviation seeking,
When but one salve relieves him!
For ev'ry simple, ev'ry herb we search
And hunt wide through the world,
When helps but one thing —
And but one man.

FIRST KNIGHT.

Expound us that?

GURNEMANZ
(evasively).

See to the bath!

FIRST ESQUIRE.
(as he turns away towards the back with the second ESQUIRE
looking off R.)

Behold yon frenzied horsewoman!

SECOND ESQUIRE.

Hey!
The mane of the devil's mare flyeth madly!

FIRST KNIGHT.
Aye! Kundry 'tis.

SECOND KNIGHT.
With news she surely cometh?

FIRST ESQUIRE.
The mare is tottering.

SECOND ESQUIRE.
Did she fly through air?

FIRST ESQUIRE.
No wowly she grovels.

Second Esquire.

Mark her mane that brushes the moss.

First Knight.

The wild witch has swung herself off.

Kundry rushes in hastily, almost reeling. Wild garb fastened up high; girdle of snakeskin hanging long, black hair flowing in loose locks; dark brownish red complexion, piercing black eyes, sometimes wild and blazing, but usually fixed and glassy. — She hurries to Gurnemanz and presses upon him a small crystal flask.

Kundry.

Here, take it! — Balsam!

Gurnemanz.

From whence bringest thou this?

Kundry.

From farther hence than thy thought can guess;
  If this balsam fail,
    Arabia bears
Nought else that can give him ease. —
Ask no farther! — I am weary.

(She throws herself on the ground.)

A train of Esquires and Knights appears L., bearing and attending the litter in which Amfortas lies stretched out. — Gurnemanz immediately turns away from Kundry towards the newcomers.

Gurnemanz
(while the procession is entering).

He comes: by faithful servants carried. —
Alas! How can mine eyes have power
To see, in manhood's stately flower,
This sov'reign of the staunchest race
To stubborn sickness made a slave!

(to the Esquires.)

Be heedful! Hark, your master groans.

(They stop and set down the litter.)

Amfortas
(raising himself slightly).

Tis well! — My thanks! — Remain awhile. —

From madd'ning tortured nights
Fair morn to woods invites:
   Sure even me
The lake's pure wave will freshen;
   My pain will flee
And tortured nights' oppression. —
Gawaine!

FIRST KNIGHT.

Sire, Gawaine waited not:
For, when the healing herb,
Whose gain such toil hath needed,
Did disappoint thy hopes,
He to another search in haste proceeded.

AMFORTAS.

Unordered? — May he be requited
For slighting thus the Grail's commands!
O woe to him, whom foes ne'er frighted,
If he should fall in Klingsor's hands!
Let none my feelings henceforth harry:
For him, the promised one, I tarry.
   "By pity 'lightened" —
Was't not so —?

GURNEMANZ.

   'Twas so thou said'st to us.

AMFORTAS.

"The guileless Fool —"
To me he doth unveil him, —
Might I as Death but hail him!

GURNEMANZ.

But first behold: accord to this a trial.
(He hands him the flask.)

AMFORTAS
(regarding it).

From whence this wondrous looking flask?

GURNEMANZ.

'Twas brought for thee from Araby afar.

AMFORTAS.

Who went to win it?

GURNEMANZ.
'Twas she, yon woman wild.

Up, Kundry! come!
(She refuses.)

AMFORTAS.
Thou, Kundry?

Mak'st me again thy debtor,
Thou restless, fearful maid? —
Well then!
Thy l alsam, ·I will even try,
In gratitude for thy good service.

KUNDRY
(moving uneasily on the ground).

No thanks! — Ha ha! What will it help thee?
No thanks! — Go, go! Thy bath!

AMFORTAS gives the sign to proceed; the procession disappears
towards the valley. — GURNEMANZ, sadly looking after, and KUNDRY
still crouching on the ground, remain. — ESQUIRES pass to and fro.

THIRD ESQUIRE
(a young man).

Hey! Thou there! —
Why liest thou thus like a savage beast?

KUNDRY.

Are not beasts here safe and sacred?

THIRD ESQUIRE.

Aye; but if thou art so,
We know not for certain yet.

FOURTH ESQUIRE
(also a young man).

With her enchanted drugs, I ween,
She'll bring destruction soon to our Master.

GURNEMANZ.

Hm! — Hath she done harm to ye? —
　When all are sore perplext
For ways to send tidings to distant lands,
　Where warrior brethren are battling,
　Their whereabouts scarcely known —
Who, ere ye are even resolved,
Starts and dashes thither and back,
The charge fulfilling with faith and knack?
She needs ye not, she's nigh you ne'er,
　Nought common hath she with you;
But when ye need help in danger time,
She breathes the breath of zeal through your
　　　　　　　　　　　　　ranks,
And never wants a word of thanks.
　If only thus she harm ye,
　It need not so much alarm ye.

THIRD ESQUIRE.

　　She hates us, though. —
See there, how hellishly she looks at us!

FOURTH ESQUIRE.

'Tis a Pagan, sure; a sorceress.

GURNEMANZ.

Yea, under a curse she may have been:
　　Here now's her home, —
　　Renewed become,
That of her sins she may be shriven
From former life yet unforgiven,
Seeking her shrift by such good actions
As advantage all our knightly factions.
Sure she does well in working thus:
Serves herself and also us.

THIRD ESQUIRE.

Then is it not surely her fault
So much distress hath come on us?

GURNEMANZ.

Aye, when she often stayed afar from us
Then broke misfortune ever in.
  I long have known her now;
  But Titurel knew her yet longer:
When he yon castle consecrated,
He found her sleeping in this wood,
  All stiff, rigid, like death.
Thus I myself did find her lately,
Just when the trouble came on us
Which yonder miscreant beyond the mountain
So shamefully did bring about. —

(to KUNDRY).

Hey, thou! — Hearken and say:
Where wert thou wandering around
When our commander lost the spear?

(KUNDRY is silent.)

Wherefore didst thou not help us then?

KUNDRY.

I never help.

FOURTH ESQUIRE.
She says't herself.

THIRD ESQUIRE.

If she 's so true and void of fear,
Then send her to search for the missing spear.

GURNEMANZ
(gloomily).

That is quite diff'rent! —
'Tis denied to all. —

(with deep emotion)

Oh, wounding, wonderful
and hallowéd spear!
I saw thee swayed
by th' unholiest hand! —

(becoming lost in remembrance)

When thus equipped, Amfortas, all too bold one,
    Who could thine arm be staying
    Th' enchanter from essaying?
While near the walls, from us the king was ta'en:
A maid of fearful beauty turned his brain.
    He lay bewitched, her form enfolding,
    The spear no longer holding: —
    A deathly cry! — I rushed anigh; —
    But laughing, Klingsor fled before;
    The sacred spear away he bore.
1 fought to aid the flying king's returning;
A fatal wound, though, in his side was burning.
That wound it is which none may make to close.

THIRD ESQUIRE.

Thou knewest then Klingsor?

GURNEMANZ
(to the 1st and 2nd ESQUIRES who come from the lake).
    How fares the king now?

SECOND ESQUIRE.
Refreshed by 's bath.

FIRST ESQUIRE.
    The balsam soothes the smart.

GURNEMANZ
(after some silence.)
That wound it is which none may make to close.

THIRD ESQUIRE.
But look ye now, father, I 'd like to know: —
Thou knewest Klingsor: how was that so?
(The third and fourth ESQUIRES have now seated themselves at
GURNEMANZ' feet; the other two do likewise).

GURNEMANZ.
Titurel, the pious lord,

He knew him well;
For, when the savage foe with craft and might
The true believers' kingdom rended,
Anon to him, in midst of holy night
The Saviour's messengers descended.
The sacred Cup, the vessel pure, unstainéd,
Which at the Last Passover Feast He drainéd, — .
Which at the Cross received His holy blood,
With eke the Spear that shed the sacred flood, —
These signs and tokens of a worth untold
The angels gave into our monarch's hold.
A house he builded for the holy things.
　　Ye, who their service have attained to
　　By paths no sinners ever gained to,
　　　Ye know 'tis but permitted
　　　The pure to be admitted
'Mid those the Grail's divinely magic power
With stength for high salvation's work doth dower.
He whom you named had therefore been denied: —
Klingsor — however long and hard he tried.
Far in yon valley then he found asylum;
For over there 'tis rankest Pagan land.
I ne'er found out what sin he had committed;
Absolved he now would be, yea holy even.
Unable in himself to stifle thoughts of evil,
　　He set to work with guilty hand,
　　Resolved to gain the Grail's command;
But with contempt was by its guardian spurned.
Wherefore in rage hath Klingsor surely learn'd
　　How by the damnable act he wrought
　　An infamous magic might be taught;
　　　Which now he's found: —
The waste he hath transformed to wondrous gardens
　　Where women bide, of charms infernal;
Thither he seeks to draw the Grail's true wardens
　　To wicked joys and pain eternal.
　　Those who are lured find him their master:
　　To many happens such disaster. —

When Titurel decayed in manhood's power
And with the regal might his son did dower
   Amfortas gave himself no rest,
    But sought to quell this magic pest;
    The sequel ye have all been told;
    The spear is now in Klingsor's hold.
Even the holy it can cleave asunder:
The Grail already he counts as his plunder.
(During the above KUNDRY has several times turned round
quickly in angry unrest).

FOURTH ESQUIRE.

Behoves us then that spear soon to reclaim.

THIRD ESQUIRE.

Ha! he who could would get both joy and fame.

GURNEMANZ
(after a silence.)

   Before the plundered sanctuary
   In pray'r impassioned knelt Amfortas,
   Imploring for a sign of safety:
A heav'nly radiance from the Grail then floated;
    A sacred phantom face
    From lips divine did chase
These words, whose purport clearly could be
                  noted: —
     "By pity 'lightened
     A guileless Fool; —
     Wait for him
     My chosen tool."
(The four ESQUIRES with deep awe repeat the oracular words.)
From the lake come cries and exclamations of the

KNIGHTS AND ESQUIRES.

Woe! Horror! — Hoho!
Up! Who is the culprit?

GURNEMANZ and the four ESQUIRES start up and turn round in
alarm. A wild swan flutters feebly from over the lake, strives to
keep up, and finally sinks dying to the ground. Meanwhile: —

GURNEMANZ.

What is 't?

FIRST ESQUIRE.

There!

SECOND ESQUIRE.

Here — a swan!

THIRD ESQUIRE.

A poor wild swan!

FOURTH ESQUIRE.

It hath been wounded.

OTHER ESQUIRES
(rushing on from the lake).

Ha! Horror! Woe!

GURNEMANZ.

Who shot the swan?

SECOND KNIGHT
(advancing).

The king esteemed it a happy token,
When over the lake it circled aloft:
Then flew a dart, —

MORE ESQUIRES
(bringing forward PARSIFAL).

He 'twas! He shot! Here's the weapon.
See this arrow, like his own.

GURNEMANZ
(to PARSIFAL).

Is't thou, that dealt this swan its death blow?

PARSIFAL.

For sure; in flight I hit all that flies.

GURNEMANZ.

This thou hast done? And hast no sorrow for
thy deed?

THE ESQUIRES.

Punish the culprit!

GURNEMANZ.

Unconceived of fact!
Couldst thou do murder? Here in holy forests,
  Whose quiet peace o'erspreads thy path?
The beasts around, didst thou not find them tame?
  Were they not friendly and fond?
  From the branches what warbled the birds to
                                            thee?
  How harmed thee that goodly swan?
To look for his mate he flew aloft,
With her to hover over the lake,
Thus consecrating for us the health giving-bath.
  Thou didst not revere, but lusted for
  A wild puerile shot of the bow.
  He was our joy: what is he to thee?
  Here — behold! — thy arrow struck; —
There stiffens his blood; hang pow'rless the pinions,
  The snowy plumage darkly besplashed, —
  Extinguished his eye; — mark'st thou its look?
  Art thou now conscious of thy trespass?
(PARSIFAL has listened to his words with increasing attention;
he now breaks his bow and casts his arrows away).
Say, boy? Perceivest thou thy heinous sin?
(PARSIFAL draws his hand across his eyes.)
How couldst thou have acted thus?

PARSIFAL.

I knew not 'twas wrong.

GURNEMANZ.

Whence comest thou?

PARSIFAL.

I do not know.

GURNEMANZ.

Who is thy father?

PARSIFAL.
I do not know.

GURNEMANZ.
Who bade thee wander this way?

PARSIFAL.
I know not.

GURNEMANZ.
Thy name then?

PARSIFAL.
I once had many,
But now I know not one of them.

GURNEMANZ.
Thou know'st not anything?
(aside)
A dolt so dull
I never found, save Kundry here.
(to the ESQUIRES who have assembled in still greater numbers.)
Now go
Nor leave the king in his bath alone! — Help.
(The ESQUIRES lift up the swan reverently and bear it away towards the lake.)

GURNEMANZ
(turning again to PARSIFAL).
Now say! Nought know'st of all I have asked thee;
Declare then what thou know'st:
Of something must thou have knowledge.

PARSIFAL.
I have a mother; Heart's Affliction she's hight:
The woods and the waste of moorlands were
our abode.

GURNEMANZ.
Who gave thee that weapon?

PARSIFAL.
I made it myself,
To drive the savage eagles from the forest.

PARSIFAL.   2

GURNEMANZ.

But eagle-like seem'st thyself, and well descended:
Why did thy mother not teach thee
Manlier weapons to handle?
(PARSIFAL remains silent).

KUNDRY
(Who, still crouching by the wood, has glanced sharply at PARSIFAL
now breaks in with hoarse tones).

Bereft of father his mother bore him,
For in battle perished Gamuret:
From like untimely hero's death
To save her offspring, strange to arms
She reared him a witless fool in deserts. —
What folly!
(she laughs).

PARSIFAL
(who has listened with sharp attention).

Aye, and once along the hem of the wood,
Most noble beasts bestriding,
Passed by men all a-glitter;
Fain had I been like them;
With laughter they galloped away.
Now I pursue, but cannot as yet o'ertake them;
Through deserts I 've wandered, o'er hill and
dale;
Oft fell the night, then followed day:
My bow was forced to defend me
'Gainst the wolves and migthy peoples.

KUNDRY
(warmly).

Yes, caitiffs and giants fell to his might;
The fierce-striking boy brings fear on their spirits.

PARSIFAL.

Who feareth me, say?

KUNDRY.
The wicked.

PARSIFAL.

Those who attacked me, were they then bad?
(GURNEMANZ laughs).
Who is good?

GURNEMANZ
(earnestly).

Thy dear mother, whom thou forsookest,
And who for thee must now mourn and grieve.

KUNDRY.

She grieves no more; for his mother is dead.

PARSIFAL
(in fearful alarm).

Dead? — What, my mother? — who says so?

KUNDRY.

I rode along and saw her dying;
    Poor fool, she sent thee her blessing.
(PARSIFAL springs upon KUNDRY, raging, and seizes her by the
throat.)

GURNEMANZ
(holding him back).

Insensate stripling! Outrage again? —
What harm has she done? She speaks the truth.
For Kundry lies not, and much has seen.
    (After GURNEMANZ has released KUNDRY, PARSIFAL stands
awhile as if turned to stone; then he is seized with a violent
trembling.)
PARSIFAL.

    I — am fainting!
(KUNDRY has hastily sprung to a brook, brings water now in
a horn, sprinkles PARSIFAL with some and then gives him to drink.)

GURNEMANZ.

'Tis well! Thus has the Grail directed:
He ousteth ill who doth give for it good.

KUNDRY
(sadly turning away.)

I do no good thing; — but rest I long for.

2 *

(Whilst Gurnemanz is attending to Parsifal with fatherly care, Kundry, unperceived by them, crawls towards a thicket).

But rest, but rest! Alas, I'm weary! —
Slumber! — Oh, would that none might wake me!
(starting timidly.)
No! I'll sleep not! — Terror grips me.

(She gives a suppressed cry and falls into a violent trembling: then she lets her arms drop powerless, and her head sink low, and staggers a little farther).

Vain to resist! The time has come.
Slumber — slumber —: I must.

(She sinks down behind the thicket and is seen no more. A stir is perceived down by the lake, and the train of Knights and Esquires with the litter passes back homewards at back).

GURNEMANZ.

From bathing comes the king again;
   High stands the sun now:
Let me to the holy Feast then conduct thee;
   For — an thou 'rt pure,
Surely the Grail will feed and refresh thee.

(He has gently laid Parsifal's arm on his own neck, and, supporting his body with his arm leads him slowly along).

PARSIFAL.

What is the Grail?

GURNEMANZ.

     I may not say:
But if to serve it thou be bidden,
Knowledge of it will not be hidden. —
   And lo! —
Methinks I know thee now indeed:
No earthly road to it doth lead,
By no one can it be detected
Who by itself is not elected.

PARSIFAL.

   I scarcely move, —
Yet swiftly seem to run.

GURNEMANZ.

My son, thou seest
Here Space and Time are one.

Gradually, while PARSIFAL and GURNEMANZ appear to walk,
the scene changes imperceptibly from L. to R. The forest disappears; a door opens in rocky cliffs and conceals the two; they
are then seen again in sloping passages which they appear to
ascend. — Long sustained trombone notes softly swell, approaching
peals of bells are heard. — At last they arrive at a mighty hall,
which loses itself overhead in a high vaulted dome down from
which alone the light streams in. — From the heights above the
dome comes the increasing sound of chimes.

GURNEMANZ
(turning to PARSIFAL who stands spell bound).

Now give good heed, and let me see,
If thou'rt a Fool and pure,
What wisdom thou presently canst secure. —

At each side in the background a large door opens. From
the R. enter slowly the KNIGHTS of the GRAIL in solemn procession,
and range themselves, during the following chorus, by degrees at
two long covered tables which are placed endways towards the
audience, one on each side, leaving the middle of the stage free.
Only cups — no dishes — stand on them.

THE KNIGHTS OF THE GRAIL.

The Holy Supper duly
Prepare we day by day,
As on that last time truly
The soul it still may stay.
Who lives to do good deeds
This Meal for ever feeds;
The Cup his hand may lift
And claim the purest gift.

VOICES OF YOUNGER MEN
(coming from the mid-height of the hall).

As anguished and lowly
His life stream's spilling
For sinners He did offer,
For the Saviour holy
With heart free and willing

My blood I now will proffer.
His body, given our sins to shrive,
Through death becomes in us alive.

BOY'S VOICES
(From the summit of the dome).

His love endures,
The dove upsoars,
The Saviour's sacred token.
Take the wine red,
For you 'twas shed;
Let Bread of Life be broken.

Through the opposite door AMFORTAS is brought in on his litter
by ESQUIRES and serving brethren; before him march boys who
bear a shrine draped in a purple-red cloth. This procession wends
to the centre of the background, where, overhung by a canopy
stands a raised couch. On this AMFORTAS is placed; before it
stands an altar-like, longish marble table, on which the boys place
the shrine, still covered. —

When the song is ended and the KNIGHTS have all taken their
seats there is a long pause and silence. — From the distant back
is heard, from an arched niche behind AMFORTAS' throne, as from
a grave, the voice of old

TITUREL.

My son Amfortas! Art at thy post?
(Silence.)
Shall I again look on the Grail and quicken?
(Silence.)
Must I perish, unguided by my Saver?

AMFORTAS
(in an outburst of painful desperation).

Woe's me! Woe, alas, the pain! —
My father, oh once again
Assume the office thou!
Live on! Live and let me perish.

TITUREL.

Entombed I live still, by the Grace of God;
Too feeble am I now to serve Him:

In works for Him thy guilt efface! —
Uncover the Grail!

AMFORTAS
(restraining the boys).

No! Leave it unrevealed! — Oh! —
May no one, no one know the anguish dire
Awaked in me by that which raptures ye! —
What is the wound and all its torture wild,
'Gainst the distress, the pangs of hell,
In this high post — accurst to dwell! —
Woeful inheritance on me pressèd,
I, only sinner 'mid the blessèd,
The holy house to guard for others
And pray for blessings upon my purer brothers! —
Oh chast'ning — chast'ning dire! descended
From — ah! the Almighty One offended.
For grace and for compassion yearning
My panting heart is riven;
In deepest soul's repentance burning
By Him to be forgiven.
The hour is nigh —
The ray descends upon the vessel divine; —
The veil is raised,
The sacred stream that in the crystal flows
With strength and radiant lustre glows; —
By this delight but filled with anguish sore,
The heavenly fount of blood
Into my heart I feel to pour;
My own life current's iniquitous flood
In delirious flight
Backward within me rushes:
Toward the world where sin has might
With wildest dread it gushes. —
Again it forces the door
From which now the stream doth pour,
Here through the wound, — like His 'tis here,
Inflicted by a stroke of that same spear. —

As in our Redeemer, the selfsame place,
From which with tears of blood burning
The Son of Man wept over man's disgrace
With sacred pity yearning;
And from which in me, in this sacred mountain,
While holding high gifts beyond measure,
— Our redemption's healing treasure —
The hot and sinful blood doth surge,
Ever renewed from my yearnings' fountain,
Which no expiation yet can purge.
Have mercy! Have mercy!
God of pity, oh! have mercy!
Take all I cherish,
Give me but healing,
That pure I may perish,
Holiness feeling.
(He sinks back as if unconscious.)

BOY'S VOICES
(from the dome).
"By pity 'lightened,
The guileless Fool —
Wait for him,
My chosen tool."

KNIGHTS
(softly).
Thus came to thee the fiat.
Wait on in hope: —
Fulfil thy duty now!

TITUREL'S
(voice).
Uncover the Grail!

AMFORTAS has again raised himself in silence. The boys uncover the golden shrine, take out of it the "Grail" (an antique
crystal cup) from which they also take a covering and set it before
AMFORTAS.

TITUREL'S
(voice).
The Blessing!

While AMFORTAS devoutly bows himself in silent prayer before the cup, an increasing gloom spreads in the room.

BOYS
(from the dome).

"Take and drink my blood;
Thus be our love remembered!
Take my body and eat:
Do this and think of me!"

A blinding ray of light shoots down from above upon the cup, which glows with increasing purple lustre. AMFORTAS, with brightened mien, raises the "Grail" aloft and waves it gently about on all sides. Since the coming of the dusk all have sunk upon their knees, and now cast their eyes reverently towards the "Grail".

TITUREL'S
(voice).

Celestial rapture!
How light now the looks of the Lord!

AMFORTAS sets down the "Grail" again, which now, while the deep gloom wanes, grows paler: the boys cover it as before and return it to the shrine. — As the original light returns to the hall the cups on the table are seen to be filled with wine, and by each is a piece of bread. All sit down to the repast including GURNE-MANZ, who keeps a place by him for PARSIFAL, whom he invites with a sign to come and partake. PARSIFAL, however remains silent and motionless at the side, as if quite dumbfounded.

(Alternative, during the Supper.)

BOYS' VOICES
(from the height).

Wine and Bread the Grail's Lord changéd
Which at that Last Meal were rangéd,
Through His pity's loving tide
When He shed for you His gore
And His Body crucified.

YOUTH'S VOICES
(from the middle height).

Blood and Body which he offered
Changed to food for you are proffered
By the Saviour ye revere

In the Wine which now ye pour
And the Bread ye eat of here.

THE KNIGHTS
(first half).

Take of this Bread,
Change it again,
Your pow'rs of body firing;
Living and dead
Strive amain
To work out the Lord's desiring.

(second half).

Take of this Wine,
Change it anew
To life's impetuous torrent;
Gladly combine,
Brothers true,
To fight as duty shall warrant.

(They rise solemnly and all join hands.)

ALL THE KNIGHTS.

Blesséd Believing!
Blesséd in Loving!

YOUTHS
(from the mid height).

Blesséd in Loving!

BOYS
(from the utmost height).

Blessed Believing!

During the repast AMFORTAS, who has not partaken, has gradually relapsed from his state of exaltation: he bows his head and
presses his hand to the wound. The pages approach him; his
wound has burst out afresh: they tend him and assist him to his
litter; then, while all prepare to break up, they bear off AMFORTAS
and the shrine in the order in which they came. The KNIGHTS
and ESQUIRES fall in and slowly leave the hall in solemn procession,
whilst the daylight gradually wanes. The bells are heard pealing
again. —

PARSIFAL, on hearing AMFORTAS' cry of agony, has clutched
his heart and remained in that position for some time; he now

stands as if petrified, motionless. When the last knight has left the hall and the doors are again closed GURNEMANZ in ill humour comes up to PARSIFAL and shakes him by the arm.

GURNEMANZ.

Why standest thou there?
Wist thou what thou saw'st?

(PARSIFAL shakes his head slightly.)

GURNEMANZ.

Thou art then nothing but a Fool!

(He opens a small side door.)

Come away, on thy road be gone
  And put my rede to use:
Leave all our swans for the future alone
  And seek thyself, gander, a goose.

(He pushes PARSIFAL out and slams the door angrily on him. As he follows the knights, the curtain closes.)

ACT II.

KLINGSOR's magic Castle. — In the inner keep of a tower open above; stone steps lead up to the battlemented summit and down into darkness below the stage, which represents the rampart. Magical implements and necromantic appliances. — KLINGSOR sits at one side on the rampart before a metal mirror.

KLINGSOR.

The time has come! —
Lo! how my magic tow'r entices
Yon Fool who neareth, shouting like a child.
A deadly slumber lays its hold on her
Whose anguish I can chase away. —
Up then! To work!

He descends somewhat lower, and lights incense, which immediately fills part of the background with a bluish vapour. He then reseats himself in his former place, and calls towards the depth with mysterious gestures:

Arise! Draw near to me!
Thy Master calls thee, nameless woman:
She - Lucifer! Rose of Hades!
Herodias wert thou, and what else?
Gundryggia there, Kundry here: —
Approach! Approach then, Kundry!
Thy Master calls — appear!

(In the bluish light rises the form of KUNDRY. She is heard to utter a dreadful cry, as if half awakened from a deep sleep.)

KLINGSOR.

Awak'st thou? Ha!
To my spell again
Thou succumbest now the time befits.

(The figure of KUNDRY gives forth a sudden shriek of anguish
sinking to a frightened wail.)

Say, where hast thou been roving again?
Fie! There with the knights and their crew,
Where as a brute they regarded thee?
  With me art thou not far better?
When once their chieftain thou hadst allured
                                      me —
Ha ha! — the spotless knight of the Grail —
  What drove thee again from my side?

KUNDRY

(hoarsely and in broken accents, as if striving to regain speech).

    Ah! — Ah!
    Dismal night —
Frenzy — Oh! — Fear! —
    Oh anguish! —
    Sleep, sleep —
Deepest sleep! — Death!

KLINGSOR.

Some other there has waked thee? Hey?

KUNDRY

(as before).

    Yes! — My curse —
Oh! Yearning — yearning!

KLINGSOR.

Ha ha! — there with the knights unsullied?

KUNDRY.

I — I — served them.

KLINGSOR.

Aye, aye! — To make some reparation,
  For the arrant wrong thou hast wrought.
    They give thee no help;
    All may be purchased,
  When I but bid their price;
    The firmest one fails,

When thy arms are around him:
And so he falls by the spear,
Which from their chief himself I purloined. —
The most dangerous must to-day be withstood:
Whom sheerest Folly shields.

KUNDRY.

I — will not! — Oh! — Oh!

KLINGSOR.

Well wilt thou, for thou must.

KUNDRY.

Thou — never — canst — hold me.

KLINGSOR.

But I can force thee.

KUNDRY.
Thou?

KLINGSOR.
Thy Master.

KUNDRY.
And by what pow'r?

KLINGSOR.

Ha! Because against me
Thine own pow'r — cannot move.

KUNDRY
(laughing harshly).

Ha, ha! Art thou chaste?

KLINGSOR
(wrathfully).

Why askest that, thou outcast wretch?
(he sinks into gloomy brooding).
Awfullest strait! —
So laughs now the Fiend below,

That once I sought the holier life!
Awfullest strait!
Irrepressible yearning woe!
Terrible lust in me once rife,
Which I had quenched with devilish strife; —
Mocks and laughs it at me,
Thou devil's bride, through thee? —
Have a care!
One his contempt and scorn hath repented;
The stern one, strong in holiness,
By whom I once was spurned
His stock I've ruined:
Unredeemed
Shall the Relics' curator soon languish;
And soon — I feel it —
I shall possess the Grail. —
Ha! ha!
How suited thy taste Amfortas the brave,
Whom to thee in rapture I gave?

KUNDRY.

Oh! — Mis'ry — Mis'ry!
Weak e'en he! Weak — all men!
By my curse and with me
All of them perish! —
Oh, unending sleep,
Only release,
When — when shall I win thee?

KLINGSOR.

Ha! He who spurns thee setteth thee free;
So try't with yon boy who draws near!

KUNDRY.
I — will not!

KLINGSOR.
Lo, where he climbs to the tow'r!

KUNDRY.

Oh woe's me! woe's me!
Awakened I for this?
Must I — must?

KLINGSOR
(who has ascended to the wall).

Ha! — He is fair, the stripling.

KUNDRY.

Oh! — Oh! — Woe is me! —

KLINGSOR
(winding a horn towards the outside).

Ho! ho! — My watchmen! Soldiers!
Heroes! — Up! — Foes are near!

(Increasing clash of weapons heard without.)

Hey! — How they haste to the ramparts,
    The deluded garrisoners,
To guard their engaging she-devils! —
    So! — Courage, courage!
    Haha! — He is not afraid: —
From bold Sir Ferris he's wrested his weapons;
And flashes them fiercely now at the swarm. —

(KUNDRY begins to laugh gloomily.)

How ill doth his zeal agree with those sots!
That one's lost an arm — that one his ancle.
    Haha! They waver — they're routed:
With their wounds they are all running home! —
    What welcome I'll give them! —
    Truly I wish
    That all the rabble of knights
    So might destroy one another! —
Ha! How proudly he stands on the rampart!
His countenance how smiling and rosy,
    As childlike, surprised
    On the desolate garden he looks! —

Hey! Kundry!

He turns round. KUNDRY, who has gone off into more and more extatic laughter which at last culminates in a spasmodic cry of anguish, now suddenly vanishes: the bluish light is extinguished; complete darkness reigns in the depths.

What! Gone to work?
Ha ha! the charm I know full well,
Which ever compels thee to do my behest. —
Thou there, babyish sprig!
What — though
Wise redes thou hast won —
Too young and dull,
Into my power thou'lt fall: —
When pureness has departed,
To me thou'lt be devoted.

He sinks slowly with the whole tower; at the same time the garden rises and fills the entire stage. Tropical vegetation; most luxuriant wealth of flowers; at the back it is bounded by the battlements of the castle wall on to which give sideways abutments of the castle itself (florid Arabian style) with terraces.

On the wall stands PARSIFAL looking down on the garden in astonishment. — From all sides, from the garden and from the palace rush in mazy courses lovely damsels, first singly, then in numbers; their dress is hastily thrown about them, as if they had been suddenly startled from sleep.

DAMSELS
(coming from the garden).

Here was the tumult; —
Weapons, wild exclaimings!

DAMSELS
(from the castle).

Horror! Vengeance! Up!
Where is the culprit?

SEVERAL.

My beloved is wounded!

OTHERS.

Where is my lover?

OTHERS.

I wakened alone! —
Where hath he fled to?

STILL OTHERS.

There in the palace? —
They're bleeding! Horror!
Where is the foe? —
There stands he! See —
'Tis my Ferris' sword. —
I saw't, he took us by storm. —
I heard too the master's horn.
My hero rushed on:
They all assailed him, but each one
Encountered a bloody repulse.
What boldness! what virulence!
All of them fled from him. —
Thou there! Thou there!
Why shape for us such distress?
Accurst, accurst mayst thou be!

(PARSIFAL leaps somewhat lower toward the garden.)

DAMSELS.

Ha! bold one! Dar'st thou approach us?
Why hast thou slaughtered our lovers?

PARSIFAL
(in greatest astonishment).

Ye lovely maidens, had I not to slay them,
When they endeavoured to check approach to
                                        your charms?

DAMSELS.

To us camest thou?
Sawest thou us?

PARSIFAL.

I've seen nowhere yet beings so bright:
If I said fair, would it seem right?

DAMSELS
(changing from surprise to merriment).
Then wilt thou not treat us badly?

PARSIFAL.
I could not so.

DAMSELS.
But sadly
What thou hast done has annoyed us;
Our playmates thou hast destroyed us:
Who'll sport with us now?

PARSIFAL.
That well will I.

DAMSELS
(laughing).
If thou art friendly come more nigh.
Let kindness be accorded,
And thou shalt be rewarded:
For gold we do not play,
But only for love's sweet pay.
Wouldst thou console us rightly
Then win it from us, and lightly.
Some have gone into the groves and now return in flower-
dresses, appearing like flowers themselves.

THE ADORNED DAMSELS
(severally).
Touch not the stripling! — He's for none but me. —
No! — No! — Me! — Me!

THE OTHER DAMSELS.
Ah, the minxes! — They've slily adorned them.
They also withdraw and return similarly dressed.

THE DAMSELS
(while, as if in merry childish gambols they press round PARSIFAL
in mazy figures and softly stroke his face.)
Come! Come!
Handsome stripling,

I'll be thy flower!
Sweetly dancing and rippling
Bliss unshadowed I'll shower.

PARSIFAL
(standing in their midst in quiet enjoyment).
How sweet is your scent!
Are ye then flowers?

THE DAMSELS
(still sometimes severally, sometimes together).
The garden's pride
And odour we' ve given.
In spring time we were riven;
    We here abide,
    Through sunlight and summer,
To bloom still on each comer.
Oh be but kind and true,
And grudge not the flowers their due:
If thou wilt not fondle and cherish,
We swiftly must wither and perish.

FIRST DAMSEL.
Unto thy bosom take me!

SECOND.
Thy hot brow, let me soothe it!

THIRD.
Turn thy fair cheek that I smooth it!

FOURTH.
Thy mouth give to my kisses!

FIFTH.
No, here! 'Tis I am the best.

SIXTH.
No, I! I am the sweeter.

PARSIFAL

(gently repulsing their eager advances).

Ye wild crowd of beautiful flowers,
If I am to play, ye must widen your bowers.

DAMSELS.

Why quarrel?

PARSIFAL.

'Tis your riot.

DAMSELS.

We quarrel for thee.

PARSIFAL.

Then quiet.

FIRST DAMSEL

(to the Second).

Back with you! See, he wants me.

SECOND DAMSEL.

No, me!

THIRD.

Me, rather!

FOURTH.

No, me!

FIRST DAMSEL

(to PARSIFAL).

Thou shunnest me?

SECOND.

Flyest me?

FIRST.

Art with women so wary?

SECOND.

Of thy favour chary?

SEVERAL DAMSELS.

The cold trembler! see how he cowers!

OTHERS.

Wouldst see the butterfly wooed by the flowers?

FIRST HALF.

Fool! we refuse him!

ONE DAMSEL.

I'm willing to lose him.

OTHERS.

We others will choose him.

OTHERS.

No, we! — draw near! —
No, I — here, here! —

PARSIFAL

(half angry, turns away and seeks to fly).

No more! You'll catch me not!

From a flowery arbour at side is heard

KUNDRY'S

(voice.)

Parsifal! — tarry!

The DAMSELS are startled and pause — PARSIFAL stands arrested.

PARSIFAL.

Parsifal . . .?
So once, when dreaming, my mother called me. —

KUNDRY'S

(voice.)

Here bide thee, Parsifal! —
Where joy and gladness on thee shall fall. — —

Ye frivolous wantons, leave him in peace:
　Flow'rs soon to be faded,
He came not here for your delight!
　Go home, tend the wounded:
Lonely awaits you many a knight.

THE DAMSELS

(tremblingly and resistingly departing from PARSIFAL).

Thus to leave thee, thus to sever —
　Alas! Alas, what pain!
From all we'd gladly part for ever,
　With thee but to remain. —
　　　Farewell! farewell!
　　　Thou fair one, thou proud one!
　　　Thou — Fool!

(With the last words they disapppear into the castle gently laughing.)

PARSIFAL.

Was all this — nothing but a dream?

He looks timidly to the side from whence KUNDRY's voice came.
There is now visible, the branches being withdrawn, a youthful
female of exquisite beauty — KUNDRY, in entirely altered form —
on a flowery couch and in light drapery of fantastic, somewha
Arabian style.

PARSIFAL

(still standing aloof).

Calledst thou me, who am nameless?

KUNDRY.

I named thee, foolish pure one,
　　　"Fal parsi", —
Thou, guileless Fool, art "Parsifal".
So cried, when in Arabia's land he expired,
Thy father Gamuret unto his son,
Who then the daylight had not greeted:
'Twas by this name he, dying, called thee.
Here have I tarried this but to disclose:
What drew thee here, if not desire to know?

PARSIFAL.

I saw ne'er, I pictured ne'er what here
I see, and which impresses me with awe. —
And bloomest thou too in this flower-garden?

KUNDRY.

Nay, Parsifal, thou foolish pure one!
Far — far from hence my home is: —
For thee to find me, I but tarried here.
I come from far lands, where I've noted much.
I saw the child upon its mother's breast;
Its infant lisping laughs yet in my ear:
    Though filled with sadness,
  How laughed then even Heart's Affliction,
    When, shouting gladness,
  It gave her sorrows contradiction!
In beds of moss 'twas softly nested,
She kissed it till in sleep it rested:
    With care and sorrow
The timid mother watched it sleeping;
    It waked the morrow
Beneath the dew of mother's weeping.
All tears was she, encased in anguish,
Caused by thy father's death and love:
That through like hap thou shouldst not languish,
Became her care all else above.
Afar from arms, from mortal strife and riot,
Sought she to hide away with thee in quiet.
  All care was she, alas! and fearing:
Never should aught of knowledge reach thy hearing.
Hear'st thou not still her lamenting voice,
    When far and late thou didst roam?
Ah! how she did laughingly rejoice
    To welcome thee hastening home!
When her wild arm around thee was laid,
Wert thou of kisses so much afraid? —
But thou didst not behold her pain,
    Her features anguish ridden,

When thou returnedst not again,
  And ev'ry trace was hidden.
For days and nights she waited,
  And then her cries abated;
Her pain was dulled of its smart,
  And gently ebbed life's tide;
The anguish broke her heart,
  And — Heart's Affliction — died. —

PARSIFAL

(always earnestly, finally terribly affected, sinks down at KUNDRY'S *feet, painfully overpowered.)*

Woe's me! Woe's me! What did I? Where was I?
Mother! Sweetest, dearest mother!
Thy son, thy son must be thy murderer?
Oh Fool! Thoughtless, shallow-brained Fool!
Where couldst thou have roved, thus to forget her?
    Thus, oh thus to forget thee,
    Faithful, fondest of mothers!

KUNDRY

(still reclining, bends over PARSIFAL'S *head, gently touches his fore-head and wreathes her arms confidingly round his neck.)*

    Hadst thou ne'er been distrest,
        Then consolation
    Could not have cheered thy breast.
    Let now thy bitter woe
        Find mitigation
    In joys that Love can shew!

PARSIFAL
(sadly).

My mother, my mother! Could I forget her?
Ah! must all be forgotten by me?
What have I e'er remembered yet?
But senseless Folly dwells in me!
    (He droops still lower.)

KUNDRY.

Transgression
When owned is quickly ended!

Confession
Hath Folly often mended.
Of Love oh learn the fashion
Which Gamuret once knew,
When Heart's Affliction's passion
Had fired his bosom through.
The life thy mother
Gave thee can smother
E'en death, and dulness too remove.
To thee
Now she
Sends benediction from above
In this first — kiss of Love.

(She has bowed her head quite over his, and now presses her lips
on his in a long kiss.)

PARSIFAL

(starts up suddenly with a gesture of intense terror: his looks alter
fearfully, he presses his hands tightly against his heart, as if to
repress an agonizing pain; finally he bursts out).

Amfortas! — —
The spearwound! — The spearwound! —
In me I feel it burning. —
Oh, horror! horror!
Direfullest horror!
It shrieks from out the depth of my soul.
Oh! — Oh! —
Misery! —
Lamentation! —
I saw thy wound a-bleeding: —
It bleeds now in myself —
Here — here!

(Whilst KUNDRY stares at him in wonder and alarm, he continues
madly.)

No, no! This is not the spearwound:
Let it gush blood in streams if it list.
Here! — here! My heart is ablaze!
The passion, the terrible passion,
That all my senses doth seize and sway!

Oh! — Love's delirium! —
How all things tremble, heave and quake
  With longings that are sinful!...
      (terribly quiet.)
My frozen glance stares on the sacred Cup: —
  The Holy One's blood doth glow; —
Redemption's rapture, sweet and mild,
Is trembling far through ev'ry spirit;
But in this heart will the pangs not lessen.
The Saviour's wailing I distinguished,
  The wailing — ah! the wailing
For His polluted sanctuary: —
  "Recover, save me from
  The hands that guilt has sullied!"
Thus — rang the lamentation
Through my soul with fearful loudness:
  And I — oh, Fool! — oh, coward!
To wild and childish exploits hither fled.
   (He throws himself despairingly on his knees.)
Redeemer! Saviour! Gracious Lord!
What can retrieve my crime abhorred?

KUNDRY
(whose astonishment has changed to sorrowful wonder, tries
tremblingly to approach PARSIFAL).

My noble knight! fling off this spell!
Look up! nor Love's delights repel!

PARSIFAL
(still in a kneeling posture, gazing blankly up at KUNDRY, *whilst*
she stoops over him with the embracing movements which he
describes in the following).

Aye! Thus it called him! This voice it was; —
And this the glance; surely I know it well, —
The eyeglance which smiled away his quiet. —
These lips too, — aye — they tempted him thus; —
  So bowed this neck above him, —
  So high was raised this head; —
  So fluttered these locks as though laughing, —
  So circled this arm round his neck —

So softened each feature in fondness, —!
In league with Sorrow's dismal weight,
   This mouth took from him
   His soul's salvation straight! —
    Ha! — with this kiss! —
(With the last words he has gradually risen, and now springs
  completely up and spurns KUNDRY from him.)
   Pernicious one! Get thee from me!
Leave me — leave me — for aye!

KUNDRY
(in intense grief).

   Cruel one! — Ha! —
   Felt e'er thy nature
   For one fellow creature,
Then feel now my desolation!
   Wert thou the Saver,
   Thou wouldst not waver,
But with me unite for salvation?
Through endless ages for thee I've waited,
   The Saviour — ah, so late!
   At whom I scoffed in hate. —
    Oh! —
   Couldst thou know the curse,
  Which through me, waking, sleeping,
   Through death and lifetime,
    Joy or weeping,
While ever steeled to bear fresh woes,
Endless through my being flows! —
   I saw Him — Him —
   And — mocked Him! . . .
I caught then His glance, —
I seek Him now from world to world,
   Once more to stand before Him:
   In deepest woe —
  Sometimes His eye doth seem near,
  His glance resting on me.
Returns then th' accursed laughter on me, —
A sinner sinks in my embraces!

Then laughter — laughter —,
Weep I cannot;
But only shriek
And rage and wallow
In night and madness never slaked,
From which, repentant, scarce I'd waked. —
Thou for whom shamed to death I've bided,
Thou whom I knew and, fool, derided,
Let me upon thy breast lie sobbing,
But for one hour together throbbing;
Though forced from God and man to flee,
Be yet redeemed and pardoned by thee!

PARSIFAL.
Eternally
Should I be damned with thee,
If for one hour
I forgot my holy mission,
Within thy arm's embracing! —
To thy help also am I sent,
If of thy cravings thou repent.
The solace, which shall end thy sorrow,
Yields not that spring from which it flows:
Salvation canst thou never borrow,
Till that same spring in thee shall close.
Far other 'tis — far other, aye!
For which I saw, with pitying eyes,
That brotherhood distrest and pining,
Their lives tormented and declining.
But who with certain clearness knows
The source whence true salvation flows?
Oh mis'ry! What a course is this!
Oh wild hallucination!
In such a search for sacred bliss
Thus to desire the soul's damnation!

KUNDRY.
And was it my kiss
This great knowledge conveyed thee?

If in my arms I might take thee,
'T would then a god surely make thee!
Redeem the world then, if 'tis thy aim: —
Stand as a god reveraléd;
For this hour let me perish in flame,
Leave aye the wound unhealéd.

PARSIFAL.

Redemption, sinner, I offer e'en thee —

KUNDRY.

Let me, divine one, but love thee;
Redemption then should I see.

PARSIFAL.

Love and Redemption thou shalt lack not, —
If the way
To Amfortas thou wilt shew.

KUNDRY
(breaking into a rage.)

Thou — never shalt find it!
Let the doomed one perish for ever. —
The shame seeker,
Joy-destitute,
Whom I have laughed at — laughed at —
laughed at!
Ha ha! He fell by his own good spear?

PARSIFAL.

Who dared raise against him the holy gear?

KUNDRY.

He — he —,
Who puts my laughter to flight:
His curse — ha! — doth lend me might:
For thyself the Spear doth await
If thou dost pity the sinner's fate! —
Ha! madness!
Pity! pity me, pray!

One single hour with me —
One single hour with thee —
Then, the wished-for
Path thou shalt straightway see!
(She seeks to embrace him: he thrusts her from him.)

PARSIFAL.

Begone, detestable wretch!

KUNDRY
(beats her breast and shrieks in wild frenzy).

Hither! Hither! Oh help!
Seize on the caitiff! Oh help!
Ward all the ways there!
Ward ev'ry passage! —
For, fled'st thou from hence, and foundest
All the ways of the world,
The one that thou seek'st,
That pathway ne'er shalt thou pass through!
All paths and courses,
Which from me would part thee,
Here — I curse them to thee:
Wander — wander, —
Thou whom I trust —
Thee will I give as his guide!

KLINGSOR has appeared upon the castle wall; the DAMSELS also
rush out of the castle and seek to hasten toward KUNDRY.

KLINGSOR
(poising a lance).

Halt there! I'll ban thee with befitting gear:
The Fool shall perish by his Master's spear!

He flings the spear at PARSIFAL; it remains floating over his
head: PARSIFAL grasps it with his hand and brandishes it with a
gesture of exalted rapture, making the sign of the Cross with it.

PARSIFAL.

This sign I make, and ban thy cursed magic:
As the wound shall be closed,
Which thou with this once clovest, —
To wrack and to ruin
Falls thy unreal display!

As with an earthquake the castle falls to ruins; the garden withers up to a desert: the DAMSELS lie like shrivelled flowers strewn around on the ground. — KUNDRY has sunk down with a cry. To her turns once more from the summit of the ruined wall the departing.

PARSIFAL.

Thou know'st —
Where only we shall meet again!

(He disappears. The curtain closes quickly.)

~~~~~~~~

ACT III.

In the Grail's domain. — Open, pleasant spring landscape, with flowery meadows rising towards the back. At the front is the border of a wood, which extends away R. A spring, in the foreground, by the wood: opposite, higher up, a narrow hermitage, built against a rock. Day-break. —

GURNEMANZ, now extremely aged, meanly dressed as a hermit, but with the tunic of a Knight of the Grail, emerges from the hut and listens.

GURNEMANZ.

From thence the groaning cometh. —
No animal grieves like that;
And on this, besides, — the holiest day we have. —
Methinks I recognize those rueful tones.

A low moaning is heard as of a sleeper terrified by dreams. — GURNEMANZ strides resolutely to a thicket at one side which has overgrown itself: he forcibly tears the brambles asunder, then pauses suddenly.

Ha! She — here again?
The hedge with its thorns overgrown
Has been her grave for how long? —
Up — Kundry! — Up!
The winter's fled, and Spring is here!
Awake, awake to the Spring! —
Cold — and stiff! —
This time truly I deem she's dead: —
Yet was't her groaning I heard just now?

(He drags KUNDRY, quite rigid and lifeless, out of the bushes, bears her to a grassy mound near, chafes her hands and temples, breathes on them and does his utmost to relax her stiffness. At last she revives. She is, just as in the first Act, dressed in the wild garb of a servant of the Grail; only her complexion is paler,

and the wildness has faded from her mien and bearing. — She
stares awhile at GURNEMANZ. Then she rises, settles her hair and
dress, and goes immediately like a serving maid to her work.)

GURNEMANZ.

Thou crazy wench!
Hast not a word for me?
Are these thy thanks,
When from deathly slumber
I have waked thee yet again?

KUNDRY
(bows her head slowly: then in hoarse and broken accents
murmurs).

Service . . . service! —

GURNEMANZ
(shaking his head).

Now will thy work be light!
We send no errands out since long:
Simples and herbs
Must ev'ryòne find for himself:
'Tis learnt in the woods from the beasts.

KUNDRY has meanwhile looked about her, and now perceives
the hut, and goes within.

GURNEMANZ
(looking after her in surprise).

How unlike this her step of yore!
Is this Holy morning the cause?
Oh, day of mercy unimagined!
No doubt for her salvation
Heaven through me revived
This wretch from deathly slumber.

KUNDRY comes from the hut again; she bears a water pot,
which she takes to the spring. Whilst she waits for it to fill, she
looks into the wood, and perceives some one approaching in the
distance; she turns to GURNEMANZ to point him out to him.

GURNEMANZ
(peering into the wood).

Who comes towards the sanctified stream?
In gloomy war apparel —
None of our brethren is he.

KUNDRY withdraws, with the filled pitcher, to the hut, where she busies herself. — GURNEMANZ steps aside in surprise, to observe the newcomer. — PARSIFAL enters from the wood. He is in complete black armour: with closed helmet and lowered spear he walks slowly forward, his head drooping, dreamily vacillating — he seats himself on the little knoll by the spring.

GURNEMANZ
(observes him a long while and then approaches somewhat).

Greet thee, my friend!
Art thou astray, and shall I direct thee?
(PARSIFAL shakes his head softly.)

GURNEMANZ.

And hast thou no greeting for me?
(PARSIFAL bows his head.)

GURNEMANZ.

Hey! — what? —
If by thy vow
Thou art bound to perfect silence,
So mine remindeth me
Straight to inform thee what is due. —
Here thou art in a holy place;
No man with weapons hither comes,
With shut up helmet, shield and spear.
This day, besides! Dost thou not know
What holy day hath dawned?
(PARSIFAL shakes his head.)

No? From whence com'st thou then?
What heathen darkness hast thou left
To hear not that to-day is
The ever hallowéd Good-Friday morn?
(PARSIFAL droops his head still lower.)

Quick, doff thy weapons!
Trouble not this morn the Master,
Who once did free all men from hell,
When bare of defence He bled for us.

PARSIFAL rises, after a further silence, thrusts the spear into the ground before him, lays down his sword and shield before it, opens his helmet and, taking it from his head, lays it with the

4*

other arms, and then kneels down in silent prayer before the spear
GURNEMANZ observes him with surprise and emotion. He beckons.
KUNDRY, who has now come out of the hut. — PARSIFAL raises
his eyes, in ardent prayer, towards the spear's head.

GURNEMANZ
(softly to KUNDRY).
Dost know who 'tis? ...
He who, long since, laid low the swan.
(KUNDRY confirms him by a slight nod).
For sure 'tis he!
The Fool whom in anger I dismissed?
Ha! by what path ay came he?
That Spear — I recognize!
(in great emotion).
Oh! — holiest day,
To which my happy soul awakes! —
(KUNDRY has turned away her face).

PARSIFAL
(rises slowly from his prayer, gazes calmly around, recognizes
GURNEMANZ, and stretches out his hand to him in greeting).
Thank Heaven that I again have found thee!

GURNEMANZ.
And dost thou know me too?
Dost recognize me,
So lowly bent by grief and care?
How cam'st thou here? From whence?

PARSIFAL.
Through error and through suff'ring lay my
pathway;
May I believe that I have freed me from it,
Now that this forest's murmur
Falls upon my senses,
And worthy voice of age doth welcome?
Or yet — is't new error?
All's altered here, meseemeth.

GURNEMANZ.
But say, where points the path thou seekest?

PARSIFAL.

To him, whose dire complainings
Once came to me, an awestruck Fool,
    And for whose healing surely
I must believe myself ordained.
        But — ah! —
The wished for path for aye denied me,
    I wandered at random,
Driven ever on by a curse:
        Countless distresses,
        Battles and conflicts
    Drove me far from the pathway;
    Well though I knew it, methought.
    Then hopeless despair overtook me
    To hold the holy Thing safely.
In its behalf, in its safe warding
I won from ev'ry weapon a wound;
        For 'twas forbidden
    That in battle I bore it:
        Undefiled
    E'er at my side I wore it,
    And now I home restore it.
'Tis this that gleaming hails thee here, —
    The Grail's most holy spear.

GURNEMANZ.

Oh Glory! Bounteous bliss!
Oh marvel! Beauteous, boundless marvel!
        (After he has somewhat collected himself.)
    Great knight! If 'twere a curse,
Which drove thee from thy proper path,
    Be sure it has departed.
Here art thou, in the Grail's domain;
Here waits for thee the knightly band.
    Ah! how they need the blessing,
    The blessing that thou bring'st! —
    Since that first day in which thou camest here,
    The mourning, which thou heardest then —

The anguish — sorely has increased.
Amfortas, struggling with his torture,
With the wound that tore his spirit,
Desired with reckless daring then his death:
No pray'rs, no sorrow of his comrades
Could move him to fulfil his holy office.
In shrouded shrine the Grail has long remained.
Its sin-repentant warder wishing,
Since he could perish not,
While he beheld its light,
To speed his dissolution,
And with his life to end his bitter sorrows.
The Holy Meal to us is now denied,
And common viands must content us;
Thereby hath withered all our heroes' strength:
Ne'er cometh message now,
Nor call to holy warfare from far countries;
Pale, dejected,. strays around
The crushed and leader-lacking band of knights.
Here on the woodside lone I hid myself,
For death with calmness waiting,
To which my old commander has succumbed;
For Titurel, my cherished chief,
When he no more beheld the Grail's refulgence,
Expired, — a man like others!

PARSIFAL
(flinging up his arms in intense grief).
And I — I 'tis,
Who all this woe have wrought!
Ha! what a grievous,
What a heinous guilt
Must then my foolish head
For ever be oppressed with!
If no atonement, expiation
My blindness e'er can banish!
I, who to save men was selected,
Must wander undirected;
All paths of safety from me vanish!

(He is on the point of falling, helplessly. GURNEMANZ supports
him, and allows him to sink down on the grassy knoll. — KUNDRY
has brought a basin of water to sprinkle PARSIFAL with.)

GURNEMANZ
(waving her off).

Not so! —
The holy fount itself
Befitteth more our pilgrim's bath.
I ween a mighty feat
Must he this morning finish,
Fulfil a sacred, mystic duty:
He should be pure as day;
So let his travel stains
Be now completely washed away.

They both turn PARSIFAL gently to the edge of the spring.
Whilst KUNDRY removes the greaves from his legs, and then bathes
his feet, GURNEMANZ meanwhile removing his corslet, —

PARSIFAL
(asks gently and wearily).

Shall I straight be guided unto Amfortas?

GURNEMANZ
(busying himself).

Most surely; there the Court our coming waits.
The obsequies of my belovéd chief,
Have even summoned me.
The Grail to us will once more be uncovered,
· The long negleted office
Once more performed before us —
To sanctify the sov'reign father,
Who through his son's great sin has died,
Which he now fain would expiate. —
'Tis thus Amfortas wills.

PARSIFAL
(observing KUNDRY with wonder).

Thou'st washed my feet so humbly: —
This friend besprinkles now my head.

GURNEMANZ

(taking water from the spring in the hollow of his hand, and sprinkling PARSIFAL's head).

Now blessed be, thou pure one, through pure water!
    So may all care and sin
    Be driven far from thee.

Meanwhile KUNDRY has taken a golden flask from her bosom and poured some of the contents upon PARSIFAL's feet, which she now dries on her hair, quickly unbound for the purpose.

PARSIFAL

(taking the flask from her).

Now that my feet thou'st anointed,
My head the friend of Titurel must lave;
For I to-day as king shall be appointed.

GURNEMANZ

(empties the flask completely over PARSIFAL's head, rubs it gently, and folds his hands over it).

    Aye, thus it was foretold me,
    My blessing on thy head: —
    Our king indeed behold we.
        Thou — pure one —
    Allpitying sufferer,
    Allknowing rescuer!
Thou who the sinner's sorrows thus hast suffered,
Assist his soul to cast one burden more.

PARSIFAL

(scoops up some water from the spring, unperceived, bends down to the kneeling KUNDRY and sprinkles her head).

    I first fulfil my duty thus: —
        Be thou baptised,
    And trust in the Redeemer!

(KUNDRY bows her head to the earth and appears to weep bitterly).

PARSIFAL

(turns round and gazes with gentle rapture on the woods and meadows).

How fair the fields and meadows seem to-day!—
    Many a magic flow'r I've seen,
Which sought to clasp me in its baneful twinings;

But none I've seen so sweet as here,
These tendrils bursting with blossom,
Whose scent recals my childhood's days
And speaks of loving trust to me.

GURNEMANZ.

That is Good-Friday's spell, my lord!

PARSIFAL.

Alas, that day of agony!
Now surely everything that thrives,
That breathes and lives and lives again,
    Should only mourn and sorrow?

GURNEMANZ.

    Thou see'st, that is not so.
The sad repentant tears of sinners
    Have here with holy rain
    Besprinkled field and plain,
    And made them glow with beauty.
All earthly creatures in delight
At the Redeemer's trace so bright
    Uplift their pray'rs of duty.
To see Him on the Cross they have no power:
And so they smile upon redeeméd man,
Who, feeling freed, with dread no more doth cower,
Through God's love-sacrifice made clean and pure:
And now perceives each blade and meadow-flower
That mortal foot to-day it need not dread;
For, as the Lord in pity man did spare,
    And in His mercy for him bled,
    All men will keep, with pious care,
    To-day a tender tread.
    Then thanks the whole creation makes,
    With all that flow'rs and fast goes hence,
    That trespass-pardoned Nature wakes
    Now to her day of Innocence.

(KUNDRY has slowly raised her head again, and gazes with moist
  eyes, earnestly and calmly beseeching up at PARSIFAL.)

PARSIFAL.

I saw my scornful mockers wither:
Now look they for forgiveness hither? —
Like blessed sweet dew a tear from thee too floweth:
Thou weepest — see! the landscape gloweth.

(He kisses her softly on the brow.)

(Distant bells are heard pealing, very gra lually swelling.)

GURNEMANZ.

Mid-day. —
The hour has come: —
Permit, my lord, thy servant hence to lead thee! —

GURNEMANZ has brought out a coat of mail and mantle of the
knights of the Grail, which he and KUNDRY put on PARSIFAL. The
landscape changes very gradually, as in the 1st Act, but from R.
to L. PARSIFAL solemnly grasps the Spear and, with KUNDRY,
follows the conducting GURNEMANZ. — When the wood has dis-
appeared, and rocky entrances have presented themselves in which
the three become invisible, processions of knights in mourning garb
are perceived in the arched passages; the pealing of bells ever increasing. — At last the whole immense Hall becomes visible just
as in the 1st Act, only without the tables. Faint light. The doors
open again. From one side the knights bear in TITUREL's corpse
in a coffin. From the other AMFORTAS is carried on in his litter,
preceded by the covered shrine of the Grail. The bier is erected
in the middle; behind it the throne with canopy where AMFORTAS
is set down.

(*Song of the knights during the procession.*)

FIRST TRAIN

(with the "Grail" and AMFORTAS).

To sacred place in sheltering shrine
The Holy Grail do we carry;
What hide ye there in gloomy shrine,
Which hither mourning ye bear?

SECOND TRAIN

(with TITUREL's coffin).

A hero lies in this dismal shrine
With all this heavenly strength,

To whom all things once God did entrust:
Titurel hither we bear.

FIRST TRAIN.

By whom was he slain, who by God himself
Once was ever sheltered?

SECOND TRAIN.

He sank neath the mortal burden of years,
When the Grail no more he might look on.

FIRST TRAIN.

Who veiled then the Grail's delights from his vision?

SECOND TRAIN.

He whom ye are bearing: its criminal guardian.

FIRST TRAIN.

We conduct him to-day, for here once again,
— And once more only —
He fulfilleth his office.

SECOND TRAIN.

Sorrow! Sorrow! Thou guard of the Grail!
Be once more only
Warned of thy duty to all.

(The coffin is set down on the bier, AMFORTAS placed on the
couch.)

AMFORTAS.

Aye, sorrow! Sorrow! Sorrow for me! —
With you I willingly cry;
Liefer yet would I ye'd give me death,
Atonement light for my trespass!

The coffin is opened. At the sight of TITUREL's body all burst
into a poignant cry of distress.

AMFORTAS

(raising himself high on his couch and turning to the body).
My father!
Highest venerated hero!

Thou purest, to whom once e'en angels bended!
  I only desired to perish,
  Yet — gave thee to death!
Oh! thou who now in heavenly heights
  Dost behold the Saviour's self,
Implore him to grant that his hallowed blood,
  (If once again here his blessing
  He pour upon these brothers)
  To them new life while giving,
  To me may offer — but Death!
      Death — darkness!
      Solit'ry mercy!
Take from me the horrible wound, the poison,
Stiffen the heart so tortured and rent!
  My father! I — call thee,
  Cry thou my words to Him:
"Redeemer! give to my son release!"

THE KNIGHTS
(severally, pressing towards AMFORTAS).

  Uncover the shrine! —
  Do now thine office!
  Thy father demands it; —
  Thou must, thou must!

AMFORTAS
in a paroxysm of despair springs up and throws himself amid the
knights, who draw back).

  No! — No more! — Ha!
Already is death glooming round me, —
And shall I yet again return to life?
      Insanity!
  What one in life can yet stay me?
  Rather I bid ye to slay me!
    (tears open his dress)

Behold me! — the open wound behold!
Here is my poison — my streaming blood.
Take up your weapons! Bury your swordblades

Deep — deep in me, to the hilts!
      Ye heroes, up!
Kill both the sinner and all his pain:
The Grail's delight will ye then regain!

*All have shrunk back in awe. Amfortas stands alone in
fearful ecstasy. — Parsifal, accompanied by Gurnemanz and
Kundry, has entered unperceived, and now advancing stretches
out the Spear, touching Amfortas' side with the point.*

PARSIFAL.

One weapon only serves: —
    The one that struck
Can staunch thy wounded side.

*Amfortas's countenance is irradiated with holy rapture; he
totters with emotion; Gurnemanz supports him.*

PARSIFAL.

Be whole, unsullied and absolved!
For I now govern in thy place.
    Oh, blessed be thy sorrows,
    For Pity's potent might
    And Knowledge' purest power
    They taught a timid Fool.
    The holy Spear —
Once more behold in this. —

*(All gaze with intense rapture on the spear which Parsifal
holds aloft, while he continues in inspiration as he looks at its
point).*

Oh mighty miracle of bliss! —
This that through me thy wound restoreth.
With holy blood behold it poureth,
Which yearns to join the fountain glowing,
Whose pure tide in the Grail is flowing!
Hid be no more that shape divine:
Uncover the Grail! Open the shrine!

*The boys open the shrine; Parsifal takes from it the "Grail"
and kneels, absorbed in its contemplation, silently praying. The
"Grail" glows with light; a halo of glory pours down over all. —
Titurel, for the moment reanimated, raises himself in benediction
in his coffin. — From the dome descends a white dove and hovers
over Parsifal's head. He waves the "Grail" gently to and fro*

before the upgazing knights. KUNDRY, looking up at PARSIFAL, sinks slowly to the ground, dead. AMFORTAS and GURNEMANZ do homage on their knees to PARSIFAL.

ALL

(with voices from the middle and extreme heights, so soft as to be scarcely audible.)

Wondrous work of mercy:
Salvation to the Saviour!

(The Curtain closes.)

~~~~~~~~~

Printed by F. A. Brockhaus, Leipzig.

PARSIFAL.

Ein Bühnenweihfestspiel.

Für Gesang:

M. Pf.

Vollständ. Clavierauszug m. Text von JOSEF RUBINSTEIN n. 30 —
   id.   id.   Erleichterte Bearbeitung (Deutscher
und englischer Text) gr. 8° . . . . n. 15 —

Für Pianoforte zu 2 Händen:

Clavierauszug ohne Text von R. KLEINMICHEL. . . n. 20 —
Vorspiel, Original-Ausgabe 1 50
   id.   Erleichterte Bearbeitung von A. HEINTZ. . . 1 50
BEYER, F. Répertoire des jeunes Pianistes 1 25
CRAMER, H. Potpourri. 1 50
GOBBAERTS, L. Transcription 1 50
HEINTZ, A. Angereihte Stücke, Heft I. . . . . . . 2 —
   id.   id.   II. 2 25
   id.   id.   III. . . . . 2 —
LISZT, Fr. Feierlicher Marsch zum heiligen Gral . . 1 75
RUBINSTEIN, Jos. Musikalische Bilder:
   I. Parsifal und die Zaubermädchen . . . . 2 —
   II. Charfreitagszauber 1 75
WICKEDE, F. VON, Auswahl von Melodien und Motiven,
leichte Bearbeitung 2 25

Für Pianoforte zu 4 Händen:

BEYER, F. Revue mélodique 1 75
CRAMER, H. Potpourri 2 75
HUMPERDINK, E. Tonsätze. . . . . Complet 20 —
   Vorspiel . . . . 2 —
   Amfortas 1 50
   Das Heilthum . . . . 1 —
   Der Schwan 1 25
   Einzug in die Gralsburg 2 25
   Das Liebesmahl. 2 25
   Klingsor und Parsifal 2 75
   Die Blumenmädchen 3 25
   Herzeleide 1 25
   Charfreitagszauber . . . . 2 —
   Titurel's Todtenfeier 1 75
   Die Erlösung . . . . 2 —
RUBINSTEIN, J. Musikalische Bilder:
   I. Parsifal und die Zaubermädchen 2 25
   II. Charfreitagszauber 1 75

Für 2 Pianoforte zu 4 Händen:

HUMPERDINK, E. Vorspiel. 1 75

Parsifal.
Für Pianoforte und Violine:

<table>
<tr><td></td><td></td><td colspan="2">M. Pf.</td></tr>
<tr><td>HEINTZ, A.</td><td>Charfreitagszauber, Episode</td><td>1</td><td>75</td></tr>
<tr><td>HUMPERDINK, E.</td><td>Vorspiel</td><td>1</td><td>50</td></tr>
<tr><td>MAHR, E.</td><td>Charfreitagszauber, Paraphrase</td><td>1</td><td>75</td></tr>
<tr><td>WILHELMJ, A.</td><td>Paraphrase</td><td>2</td><td>25</td></tr>
</table>

Für Pianoforte und Violoncell:

GRÜTZMACHER, Leop. Drei Stücke:

No 1. In Klingsor's Zaubergarten (Parsifal und die Blumenmädchen) 2 75
„ 2. Kundry's Erzählung . . . . 2 —
„ 3. Die Blumenaue (Charfreitagszauber). 2 25

Für Pianof., Harmonium, Violine u. Violoncell:

STEINBACH, F. Vorspiel. 3 50

Für Orgel:

HÄNLEIN, A. Vorspiel, zum Concertvortrag 1 25

Zum Concertvortrag für Orchester etc.:

Vorspiel . . . . Partitur n. 20 —
           Orchesterstimmen n. 9 25
Charfreitagszauber . . . . Partitur n. 20 —
           Orchesterstimmen n. 7 25
Verwandlungsmusik und Schluss-Scene des I. Actes für
Orchester und Chor zum Concert-Vortrage eingerichtet
           Partitur n. 30 —
           Orchesterstimmen n. 17 —
           Chorstimmen n. 1 75
   id.   id.   für Orchester allein eingerichtet
           Partitur n. 25 —
           Orchesterstimmen n. 13 —

Textbücher:

<table>
<tr><td>Parsifal.</td><td>Ein Bühnenweihfestspiel. Dichtung.</td><td>. n.</td><td>3 —</td></tr>
<tr><td>id.</td><td>id. eleg. geb. in engl. Leinwand</td><td>. n.</td><td>3 60</td></tr>
<tr><td>id.</td><td>id. Ausgabe in 16°. brochirt.</td><td>. . n.</td><td>— 80</td></tr>
<tr><td>id.</td><td>id. eleg. geb. in engl. Leinwand</td><td>. n.</td><td>1 40</td></tr>
<tr><td>Parsifal.</td><td>A festival drama. Translated into English in exact accordance with the original by H. L. & F. CORDER</td><td>. n.</td><td>1 —</td></tr>
<tr><td>id.</td><td>eleg. geb. in engl. Leinwand</td><td>. n.</td><td>2 —</td></tr>
</table>

DER RING DES NIBELUNGEN.
Ein Bühnen-Festspiel für drei Tage und einen Vorabend.
Vorabend.
DAS RHEINGOLD.
Musik-Drama in 4 Scenen.

Vollständige Orchester-Partitur . . . . — —

Das Rheingold.

Für Gesang.

		M.	*Pf.*
Vollständiger Clavierauszug . . . . n.	16	75
id. id. Erleichterte Ausg. gr. 8⁰.. . n.	10	—

Einzeln daraus:

N⁰ 1.	Gesang der drei Rheintöchter (2 Sopr. & Alt). .	4	—
2.	Erda's Warnung an Wotan (Alt)	1	—
3.	Loge's Gesang „Immer ist Undank" (Tenor) .	—	75

Für das Pianoforte.

Clavierauszug zu 2 Händen . . . . n.	10	50
Clavierauszug zu 4 Händen . . . . n.	18	—
Vorspiel (Ouverture)	1	—
id. id. vierhändig	1	50
Tonbilder für das Pianoforte, mit erläuterndem, unterlegtem und verbindendem Texte . . . . n.	6	25
BEYER, F. Répertoire des jeunes Pianistes	1	25
— Revue mélodique (vierhändig)	1	75
BRASSIN, L. Walhall, frei übertragen	1	75
CRAMER, H. Potpourri	1	50
— id. (vierhändig)	2	75
— Leichte Tonstücke N⁰ 1	2	—
— id. (vierhändig)	2	75
DÖRSTLING, CL. Motive, leicht bearbeitet (vierhändig)	3	25
HEINTZ, A. Angereihte Perlen	2	—
HORN, A. Einzug der Götter in Walhall, für 2 Pianoforte zu 8 Händen	6	50
JAELL, A. Erste Scene für das Pianoforte. Op. 120	2	25
KERN, L. Reminiscenz f. Harmonium u. Pianoforte. .	3	25
LANGHANS, L. Loge's Erzählung	1	25
LISZT, F. Walhall, Transcription	1	75
GREGOIR, J. & LÉONARD, H. Duo f. Pianof. u. Violine	3	25
POPP, W. Transcription f. Flöte u. Pianoforte . . .	1	—
RUPP, H. Fantasie	3	—
STASNY, L., Tonbilder f. Orchester, op. 200. Partitur n.	12	—
Orchesterstimmen n.	20	—
WICHTL, G. Petit Duo pour Piano et Violon. op. 98	2	—
ZUMPE, H. Einzug der Götter in Walhall. Für Orchester zum Concertvortrag bearbeitet. Partitur . . . . n.	6	—
Orchesterstimmen n.	12	—

Erster Tag.

DIE WALKÜRE.

Musik-Drama in 3 Aufzügen.

Vollständige Orchester-Partitur . . . . — —

Die Walküre.

Für Gesang.

M. Pf.

Vollständiger Clavierauszug. . . . . n. 22 —
   id.   id.   Erleichterte Ausgabe, bearbeitet von
          R. KLEINMICHEL. gr. 8⁰. . n. 12 —

Einzeln daraus:

No 1. Ein Schwert verhiess mir der Vater (Tenor). . 1 —
„ 2. Winterstürme wichen dem Wonnemond (Winter-
        storms have waned) (Tenor) . . . 1 —
„ 2bis   id.   id.   (Bariton) . 1 —
„ 3. Siegmund! sieh auf mich (Sopran u. Tenor). . 2 75
„ 4. War es so schmählich, was ich verbrach! (Sopran
     und Bass) 4 25
„ 4bis Wotan's Abschied (Bass). 1 25

Für das Pianoforte.

Clavierauszug zu 2 Händen. . . . . n. 14 75
Clavierauszug zu 4 Händen . . . . n. 20 —
Vorspiel (Ouverture). . . . . 1 —
   id.   id.   vierhändig 1 75
Tonbilder für das Pianoforte, mit erläuterndem, unter-
  legtem und verbindendem Texte. In 3 Theilen, jeder n. 4 50
Der Ritt der Walküren. 1 75
   id.   id.   (vierhändig). 2 25
   id.   id.   (für 2 Pianoforte zu 4 Händen) 3 25
Wotan's Abschied und Feuerzauber. 1 75
   id.   id.   (vierhändig) 2 75
   id.   id.   Für 2 Pianoforte zu 8 Händen . . 5 75
BEYER, F. Répertoire des jeunes Pianistes 1 25
  — Revue mélodique (vierhändig) 1 75
BRASSIN, L. Tonstücke, frei übertragen,
  No 2. Siegmund's Liebesgesang. 1 50
  „ 3. Feuerzauber 1 75
  „ 4. Der Ritt der Walküren 2 75
CRAMER, H. Potpourri 1 50
  —   id.   (vierhändig) 2 75
  — Leichte Tonstücke No 2. . . . . 2 —
  —   id.   (vierhändig) 2 75
DÖRSTLING, CL. Motive, leicht bearbeitet (vierhändig) 4 —
GREGOIR, J. Transcription 1 50
HEINTZ, A. Angereihte Perlen.
  Heft 1. Erster Aufzug . . . . 2 —
    „ 2. Zweiter Aufzug. . . . . 2 —
    „ 3. Dritter Aufzug 2 75
  — Liebeslied und Zwiegesang des Wälsungen-
    paares (Siegmund und Sieglinde) . . . . 2 —

Die Walküre.

~~~~~~~~~~~

Zweiter Tag.

S I E G F R I E D.

Musik-Drama in 3 Aufzügen.

Siegfried.

Für Gesang.

Vollständiger Clavierauszug . . . . .n. 25 25
id.   id.   erleichterte Ausgabe, bearbeitet
von R. KLEINMICHEL, gr. 8⁰ . . . . n. 15 —

Einzeln daraus:

No 1.	Es sangen die Vöglein (Tenor)	—	75
„ 2.	Nothung! Nothung! Neidliches Schwert (Tenor)	1	—
„ 3.	Hoho! Hoho! Schmiede mein Hammer (Tenor)	1	—
„ 4.	Hei was ist das für ein müssiger Tand (Tenor)	1	25
„ 5.	Als zullendes Kind (Tenor).	—	75
„ 6.	Wache Wala! Wala (Bass).	3	25

Für das Pianoforte.

Clavierauszug zu zwei Händen . . . . n. 17 75
Clavierauszug zu vier Händen . . . . n. 18 —
Vorspiel (Ouverture). . . . . 1 —
Tonbilder für das Pianoforte, mit erläuterndem, unter-
legtem und verbindendem Texte . . . . n. 10 —
BEYER, F. Répertoire des jeunes Pianistes. 1 25
— Revue mélodique (vierhändig) . . . . , . 1 75
BRASSIN, L. Waldweben, frei übertragen . . . . . 2 —
CRAMER, H. Potpourri. 1 50
—   id.   (vierhändig) 2 75
— Leichte Tonstücke No 3 . . . . 2 —
    id.   (vierhändig) 2 75
HEINTZ, A. Angereihte Perlen. In vier Heften, jedes 1 75
— Siegfried's Feuerdurchschreitung und Erweckung
der Brünnhilde. Episode 2 75
JAELL, A. Transcription. Op. 146. . . . . 2 25
— Etude-Transcription. Op. 147. . . . . 1 75
PRINGSHEIM, A. Siegfried und der Waldvogel.
Episode, bearbeitet für Pianoforte, 2 Violinen, Viola
und Violoncell 6 75
RUBINSTEIN, Jos. Musikalische Bilder.
I. *Siegfried und der Waldvogel* 2 25
    id.   id.   (vierhändig) . . . 2 75
II. *Siegfried und Brünnhilde* 2 25
    id.   id.   (vierhändig) . . . 2 75
RUPP, H. Fantasie. . . . . 3 —
— Waldweben. . . . . 3 —
WICHTL, G. Petit Duo pour Piano & Violon. op. 98 2 —
Waldweben, für Orchester zum Concertvortrag einge-
richtet . . . . Partitur n. 5 —
Orchesterstimmen n. 8 —

Dritter Tag.

GÖTTERDÄMMERUNG.

Musik-Drama in 3 Aufzügen.

M. Pf.

Vollständige Orchesterpartitur . . . . — —

Für Gesang.

Vollständiger Clavierauszug . . . . n. 30 —
   id.   id.   erleichterte Ausgabe, bearbeitet
von R. KLEINMICHEL, gr. 8°. . . . . n. 15 —

Einzeln daraus:

No 1. Duett. Brünnhilde und Siegfried (Sop. u. Ten.)   2 50
„ 2. Gesang der drei Rheintöchter (2 Soprane u. Alt)   3 75

Für das Pianoforte.

Clavierauszug zu 2 Händen. . . . . n. 25 —
Clavierauszug zu 4 Händen . . . . n. 20 —
Tonbilder für das Pianoforte, mit erläuterndem, unter-
  legtem und verbindendem Texte, in 2 Theilen,
                                    Theil I. n.   6 —
                                    Theil II. n.   8 —
BEYER, F. Répertoire des jeunes Pianistes. 1 25
  — Revue mélodique (vierhändig) 1 75
CRAMER, H. Potpourri. 1 50
  —   id.   (vierhändig) 2 75
  — Leichte Tonstücke No 4 . . . .   2 —
  —   id.   (vierhändig) 2 75
HEINTZ, A. Angereihte Perlen.
      Heft I. *Vorspiel* 1 75
       „ II. *Erster Aufzug*. 2 25
       „ III. *Zweiter Aufzug* 1 75
       „ IV. *Dritter Aufzug* 2 75
JAELL, A. 1te Transcription. op. 164 . . . . . .   2 25
  —   2te Transcription. op. 165 . . . . . .   2 —
OBERTHÜR. C. Gesang der Rheintöchter, übertragen
  für Harfe und Pianoforte 2 75
RUBINSTEIN, Jos. Musikalische Bilder.
    I. *Siegfried und die Rheintöchter* . . . .   3 —
     id.   id.   (vierhändig) 3 25
RUPP, H. Fantasie . . . .   3 —
SEIDL, A. Siegfried's Rheinfahrt, Tonbild für Piano-
  forte, 2 Violinen, Viola, Violoncell und Contrabass   5 —

Götterdämmerung.

<table>
<tr><td></td><td></td><td>M. Pf.</td></tr>
</table>

Trauermarsch beim Tode Siegfried's und Brünnhilde's
Klagegesang, für die Orgel zum Concertgebrauch
übertragen von E. STEHLE 2 25
Trauermarsch beim Tode Siegfried's.

	Für grosses Orchester . . . Partitur n.		5 —
		Orchesterstimmen n.	9 —
id.	Für Pianoforte zu 2 Händen *(Cramer)* .		1 25
id.	Für Pianoforte zu 4 Händen (id.) .		1 50
id.	Für Pianoforte zu 2 Händen *(Heintz)* . .		1 50
id.	Für Pianoforte zu 4 Händen (id.) .		1 75
id.	Für 2 Pianoforte zu 4 Händen *(Ehrlich)*.		2 75
id.	Für 2 Pianoforte zu 8 Händen *(Rupp)*. .		3 —
id.	Für Pianoforte und Violine *(Hermann)* .		2 50
id.	Für Pianoforte und Violoncell (id.) .		2 50

Siegfried's Tod und Trauermarsch, für kleineres Orchester
bearbeitet von L. STASNY . . . . Partitur n. 4 50
                                   Orchesterstimmen n. 7 —
Siegfried's Tod und Trauermarsch für Pianoforte,
2 Violinen, Viola und Violoncell von A. PRINGSHEIM 3 50
WICHTL, G. Petit Duo pour Piano & Violon. op. 98 2 —
ZUMPE, H. Siegfried's Rheinfahrt, eingerichtet für
Pianoforte, Violine und Violoncell 4 25
— Gesang der Rheintöchter, zum Concertvortrage
eingerichtet. . . . . Partitur n, 7 50
                                   Orchesterstimmen n. 12 50

DIE MEISTERSINGER VON NÜRNBERG.

Oper in 3 Acten.

Vollständige Orchester-Partitur. . . . . — —

Für Gesang.

Vollständiger Clavierauszug von KARL TAUSIG . . . n. 31 50
  id.   id.   Erleichterte Ausgabe bearbeitet
von R. KLEINMICHEL. gr. 8⁰. . . . . n. 15 —

Einzeln daraus:

No 1. Pogner's Anrede, für Bass. 1 25
„ 2. Walther vor der Meisterzunft (deutsch-französisch)
        für Tenor. . . . . 1 —
      id.   id.   (deutsch-englisch) . . 1 —
„ 2bis id.   id.   Ausgabe für Bariton
                      (deutsch-englisch) 1 —

VIII

Die Meistersinger von Nürnberg.

~~~~~~

Für das Pianoforte.

Zweihändig.

Die Meistersinger von Nürnberg.

Die Meistersinger von Nürnberg.

Für Orgel.

Für Harmonium.

Die Meistersinger von Nürnberg.

Für Harfe.

M. Pf.

OBERTHÜR, C. Walthers Preislied 1 50

Zum Concertvortrag für Orchester etc.

Vorspiel (Ouverture), Partitur . . . . n. 5 50
id.   id.   Stimmen . . . . n. 9 50
id.   für grosses Militär-Orchester, bearbeitet von
     A. ABBASS, Partitur . . . . n. 5 75
id.   id.   Stimmen . . . . n. 13 25
id.   (Einleitung) des dritten Actes, Tanz der Lehr-
     buben, Aufzug der Meistersinger und Gruss
     an Hans Sachs . . . . Partitur n. 6 —
             Orchesterstimmen n. 16 50
Apotheose des Hans Sachs, für Orchester und ge-
     mischten Chor   Partitur n. 10 —
             Orchesterstimmen n. 5 —
             Chorstimmen n. — 75
STASNY, L. Potpourri für kleines Orchester 7 25

Textbücher.

Einzeln:

Fünf Gedichte.

Für eine Frauenstimme mit Begleitung des Pianoforte.

Für Sopran 3 25
Für eine tiefere Stimme 3 25

Richard Wagner.

Einzeln:

		M.	Pf.
№ 1.	Der Engel (The Angel)	—	75
„ 2.	Stehe still (Stand still)	1	—
„ 3.	Im Treibhaus (In the Hothouse) . .	—	75
„ 4.	Schmerzen (Pains)	—	50
„ 5.	Träume (Dreams)	—	75

Träume (aus den fünf Gedichten) für Violine mit
Orchesterbegleitung . . . . n. 4 —

id. für Violine (od. Violoncell, od. Flöte, od.
Clarinette, od. Hoboe) mit Pianofortebegl. n. 1 50

id. für Orchester bearbeitet von L. STASNY n. 6 —

LÉONARD, H. Fünf Gedichte, übertragen für Violine
und Pianoforte 3 25

Huldigungs-Marsch
für
Ludwig II. König von Bayern.

Für grosses Orchester.

Partitur n. 4 25

In Stimmen n. 10 50

Für das Pianoforte 1 50

Für das Pianoforte übertragen von H. von BÜLOW . . 1 50

Für das Pianoforte übertragen id. (vierhändig) . . 2 —

Für 2 Pianoforte zu 8 Händen 3 50

Grosser Festmarsch

Zur Eröffnung der hundertjährigen Gedenkfeier der
Unabhängigkeits-Erklärung der vereinigten Staaten von
Nordamerika.

Für grosses Orchester.

Partitur n. 15 —

In Stimmen n. 15 —

Für das Pianoforte übertragen von JOSEPH RUBINSTEIN . 3 50

Für das Pianoforte. Erleichterte Ausgabe 2 50

Für das Pianoforte. Zu vier Händen. 3 50

Richard Wagner.

Siegfried-Idyll.

Für Orchester.

	M. Pf.
Partitur n.	10 —
Orchesterstimmen n.	8 —
Für Pianoforte, 2 Violinen, Viola und Violoncell eingerichtet von A. PRINGSHEIM	6 25
Für Pianoforte, Violine, Violoncell und Harmonium (oder 2tes Pianoforte) einger. von P. DRUFFEL . . .	5 50
Klavier-Auszug zu 2 Händen von JOSEPH RUBINSTEIN .	3 50
id. zu 4 Händen.	4 25

Album - Sonate

Für das Pianoforte	3 —
Für Orchester bearbeitet von C. MÜLLER-BERGHAUS	
Partitur n.	6 —
Orchesterstimmen n.	10 —

Albumblatt

(Frau Betty Schott gewidmet)

Für das Pianoforte	1 50
Für Violine mit Orchester- oder Pianoforte-Begleitung von E. SINGER . . . . .Partitur	2 —
Mit Begleitung des Orchesters	5 75
Mit Begleitung des Pianoforte	2 25
Für Viola und Pianoforte einger. von H. RITTER . . .	1 75
Für Violoncell und Pianof. einger. von G. GOLTERMANN	1 75

Die beiden Grenadiere.

Gedicht von H. Heine.

Für eine Singstimme mit Begleitung des Pianoforte . .	1 25

Nibelungen-Marsch von G. Sonntag.

Mit Benutzung der Fanfaren zu den Bayreuther Bühnen-Festspielen.

Für Infanterie-Musik . . . . Partitur n.	2 50
Für das Pianoforte	1 —

Ferner erschienen nachstehende billige Octav-Ausgaben von Opern-Auszügen für Gesang und Pianoforte mit deutschem und französischem Texte:

Kammermusik:
Neue empfehlenswerthe Werke.

D. ALARD. Les Maîtres classiques du Violon. Collection de Morceaux choisis dans les Chefs-d'Oeuvres des plus grands Maîtres classiques avec le style, le phrasé, l'expression, les doigtés et le coup d'archet, pour Violon et Piano.

New Catalogues of Violin Music Post-free on application to the Publishers SCHOTT & CO. 159, Regent Street, LONDON, W.

NEW AND POPULAR
PIANOFORTE SOLOS.

SYDNEY SMITH:

				s.	d.
Réveil du Printemps. Op. 199.				4	0
Danse des Fantômes. Morceau dramatique. Op. 200				4	6
Sérénade Venitienne. Op. 201				4	0
La Séduisante, Valse de Salon. Op. 202				4	6
Vie Orageuse, Impromptu appassionato. Op. 203				4	0
Chant des Forgerons. Op. 204				4	0

HENRI KOWALSKI:

Autour de mon Clocher, Pastorale. Op. 44		3	6
Illusions et Chimères, Valse-Caprice. Op. 45		4	0
Chanson Cosaque. Op. 46		3	6
Sous les Tropiques, Berceuse. Op. 47		3	6
Tambour battant, Marche militaire. Op. 48		3	6
Simple Pensée, Mélodie. Op. 49		3	0

All Music half-price unless marked net.

New Catalogues of Popular Pianoforte Music,
Post-free, on application to the Publishers:

SCHOTT & CO. B. SCHOTT'S SÖHNE.
159, REGENT STREET, WEIHERGARTEN,
LONDON, W. **MAYENCE.**

SCHOTT & CO.
281, GEORGE STREET,
SYDNEY.

Printed by F. A. Brockhaus, Leipzig.

www.ingramcontent.com/pod-product-compliance
Lightning Source LLC
Chambersburg PA
CBHW030002030726
47499CB00008B/2858